UNDOCUMENTED IMMIGRANTS

CATHLEEN SMALL

LUCENT
P R E S S

Published in 2018 by
Lucent Press, an Imprint of Greenhaven Publishing, LLC
353 3rd Avenue
Suite 255
New York, NY 10010

Produced for Lucent by Calcium
Designer: Jeni Child
Picture researcher: Rachel Blount
Editors: Sarah Eason and Nancy Dickmann

Picture credits: Cover: Shutterstock: Budimir Jevtic (main), Vinokurov Kirill (top); Inside: Library of Congress: George Grantham Bain Collection 4–5, 17, 18–19, 19t, Dorothea Lange/U.S. Farm Security Administration 8, 9, Russell Lee/U.S. Farm Security Administration 7, U.S. Navy 21; Shutterstock: Nate Allred 31, Bignai 57, Bikeworldtravel 41, Marie Kanger Born 50, Divanov 43, Everett Historical 10, 14–15, 16, 22, 49, Charles Harker 42, Imagentle 38, JStone 40, Legenda 26–27, Reed Means 56, Lissandra Melo 44–45, Monkey Business Images 58–59, Susan Montgomery 46, Photographee. eu 47, Rawpixel.com 25, Gregory Reed 51b, RomanR 37, Tolga Sezgin 51, ShutterDivision 12–13, Joseph Sohm 48, Richard Thornton 30, Txking 52, Ken Wolter 35; U.S. Customs & Border Protection: Donna Burton 32–33t; Wikimedia Commons: Laton Alton Huffman 5t, Photo Courtesy of ICE 54–55, Russell Lee/U.S. Farm Security Administration 23, Rvplpr 33b, Gage Skidmore 28, U.S. Navy Photo by Photographer's Mate 2nd Class Bob Houlihan 60–61t.

Library of Congress Cataloging-in-Publication Data

Names: Small, Cathleen.
Title: Undocumented immigrants / Cathleen Small.
Description: New York : Lucent Press, 2018. | Series: Crossing the border | Includes index.
Identifiers: ISBN 9781534562233 (library bound) | ISBN 9781534562240 (ebook) | ISBN 9781534562783 (paperback)
Subjects: LCSH: Illegal aliens--United States--Juvenile literature. | Illegal aliens--Government policy--United States--Juvenile literature. | United States--Emigration and immigration--Juvenile literature.
Classification: LCC JV6483.S63 2018 | DDC 364.1'37--dc23

Printed in the United States of America

CPSIA compliance information: Batch #CW18KL: For further information contact Greenhaven Publishing LLC, New York, New York at 1-844-317-7404.

Please visit our website, www.greenhavenpublishing.com. For a free color catalog of all our high-quality books, call toll free 1-844-317-7404 or fax 1-844-317-7405.

CONTENTS

CHAPTER 1

IMMIGRATION FROM MEXICO

The United States has an estimated 11 million unauthorized immigrants living within its borders. Of those 11 million, more than half—about 6 million—are from Mexico. This is not surprising, given that Mexico shares a long border with the United States. Although there are immigration laws and border patrols to prevent people from entering, it's still possible for an immigrant to make their way over the border and into the United States. Mexican immigrants have a long and rich history in the United States.

NORTH AMERICA BEFORE EUROPEANS

But who were the first immigrants in North America? Long before settlers began to arrive from Europe and elsewhere, Native Americans lived throughout the land that now makes up the United States. They are thought to have first arrived in the Americas around 12,000 years ago—which is much, much longer than the four or five centuries since Europeans first arrived to explore and settle.

Mexican citizens have been immigrating to the United States for centuries.

Native Americans had many different complex cultures. They did not have a centralized government that covered all tribes in North America. Many tribes were nomadic hunter-gatherers, while others practiced agriculture.

Europeans colonized North America, often using violence and military force to take land that had been occupied by Native Americans. Europeans also carried diseases to the Americas, which caused epidemics and killed large numbers of Native Americans.

Today, the United States government officially recognizes more than 560 Native American tribes and bands.

THE FIRST UNDOCUMENTED IMMIGRANTS

The United States became an independent country in 1776. Some of the earliest undocumented immigrants in U.S. history were probably U.S.

citizens who were trying to move into territory that was owned by Mexico! Mexico won independence from Spain in 1821, and the land that is now Texas became part of Mexico. At first, Mexico allowed U.S. citizens to settle in Texas, but it wasn't long before white settlers outnumbered the Mexicans living there. Mexico banned immigration from the United States in 1830, but soon there were nearly four times as many U.S. citizens living in the region as there were Mexicans. Some American citizens lied to Mexican authorities by saying they had work to complete and would leave the territory within 20 days, after the work was complete. Many of these citizens did not live up to their end of the agreement.

CHANGING BORDERS

In the mid-nineteenth century, American citizens wanted to expand westward, settling in Texas and beyond. The United States annexed Texas in 1845, which resulted in the Mexican-American War (1846-1848) due to a dispute over Texas's borders. Mexico argued that Texas ended at the Nueces River, and the United States argued that it reached the Rio Grande. Through the war, the United States acquired 500,000 square miles (1,300,000 square km) of Mexican territory. Now, the United States extends to the Pacific Ocean and can expand no farther west.

TERMINOLOGY

You may hear a lot of different terms used to refer to people who come to the United States without authorization: undocumented immigrant, unauthorized immigrant, illegal immigrant, illegal alien, undocumented alien. In general, "undocumented" or "unauthorized" are the preferred terms. An undocumented immigrant is someone who is living in a country that is not their home country without authorization.

Some people feel that the term "illegal immigrant" implies that the person has done something criminal. In reality, most undocumented immigrants have no criminal history and are simply living in the United States without authorization.

Undocumented immigrants may have arrived in the United States in different ways. They may have different reasons for why they are living here without authorization.

History of Immigrants from Mexico

Mexican citizens began immigrating to the United States in large numbers around the 1850s. Between the 1850s and the 1880s, 55,000 Mexican workers immigrated to the United States to work in agricultural jobs, the mining industry, and on the railroads. Mexican immigrants were a particularly large part of the railroad industry, with 60 percent of the crews building the United States–Mexico railroad being Mexican.

In the 1910s, the rate of immigration was around 20,000 immigrants per year. During World War I, many Mexican immigrants came to work in industry and service jobs, such as mechanics, plumbers, and machinists. By the 1920s, the number had jumped to between 50,000 and 100,000 immigrants per year.

In 1920, the Mexican government created a contract that Mexican immigrants had to sign before coming to the United States for work. The contract was countersigned by an immigration official, and it guaranteed that immigrants could bring their family with them for the duration of their contract. It also established their pay rate, work schedule, and place of employment.

Many Mexican families came to the United States to work on farms, especially at harvest time.

CREATING THE BORDER PATROL

The United States established the Border Patrol when it passed the Labor Appropriation Act of 1924. At this point, being a Mexican living in the United States without documentation became illegal, and the term "illegal alien" arose. However, Mexicans were exempt from the immigration quotas that the act established. They were seen as a necessary part of the United States' agricultural economy, so at that time, they did not face the legal discrimination that immigrants from some other areas did.

MASS DEPORTATIONS DURING THE GREAT DEPRESSION

During the Great Depression, jobs became extremely scarce. Americans grew hostile towards immigrants, whom they saw as competition for work. Any Mexican living in the United States who couldn't prove they had secure employment were deported and told not to return, under the penalty of law. Even many Mexican immigrants who had come to the U.S. legally were pressured or forced to leave. Tens of thousands of Mexican immigrants voluntarily returned to Mexico, and hundreds of thousands were deported.

Unauthorized immigrants from Mexico sometimes came across the border hidden on freight trains.

ELENA

Elena Santiago came to Arizona from Mexico without documentation in 1985, when she was almost 13 years old. She quickly got a job working on a farm alongside her mother. The pay was very low and Elena was unable to attend school. When Elena got older, she went to Phoenix and worked in several jobs using a fake name. Elena eventually had two children, who were automatically U.S. citizens because they were born in the United States.

Elena was raising her children as a single mother when a dispute with her landlord brought her to the attention of authorities. Shortly thereafter, on November 3, 2011, immigration authorities came to her home and removed Elena for deportation. Her children were put in foster care, and the family pets were left in the residence to die. When Elena refused to sign a voluntary order of deportation, immigration agents forcibly grabbed her hands and pressed a thumbprint onto the order—which was equivalent to a signature. Elena was deported to Mexico and would not see her toddler daughter, who remained in a foster home, for 14 months.

During the 1930s, jobs were scarce, both for immigrants and for U.S. citizens.

THE BRACERO TREATY

Then in 1942, the tight control on the borders relaxed when the United States passed the Bracero Treaty, which allowed millions of Mexican laborers to immigrate to the United States over the next 20 years to work in agriculture. The Bracero Program ended in 1964, when automation and an overflow of undocumented immigrants rendered the program obsolete. However, this did not slow the influx of Mexican-born immigrants. They still came to the United States to work, but with the dissolution of the Bracero Program, they came without documentation. The farmers who hired Mexican immigrants to labor in the fields continued to employ them, despite their undocumented status.

By 1933, about 15 million Americans were unemployed.

LIFE AS A BRACERO

Rigoberto Garcia came to the United States four separate times through the Bracero Program. He found that the money was decent, but the work was difficult and the conditions were harsh, at best. Garcia remembers, "A lot was always expected of you, and they always demanded even more." Garcia doesn't regret being a bracero, because, as he says, "It was the beginning of the life I'm leading now. Thanks to those experiences…here I am."

PERSONAL STORIES

NEW QUOTAS

When the Immigration and Nationality Act of 1965 was passed, it set quotas on immigration from Mexico for the first time. Starting in 1965, a quota of 20,000 Mexican immigrants per year was set. Given that totals sometimes reached up to about 50,000 Mexican immigrants per year, the quota resulted in a reduced flow of legal immigration from Mexico—and a new flow of undocumented immigration. Mexicans were still coming to the United States to work, and if they couldn't do so with documentation, many did so without documentation.

The Immigration and Nationality Act of 1965 also gave priority to immigrants entering the country to be reunited with their families. Because the Mexican immigrant population in the United States was already large, this meant that many more Mexicans entered the country. Many did so legally, and others came without authorization when they could not acquire the necessary documentation.

THE IMMIGRATION REFORM AND CONTROL ACT

In 1986, the United States government passed the Immigration Reform and Control Act, which granted amnesty to 2.7 million undocumented workers— mostly Mexican immigrants—living in the United States. The new law succeeded in bringing about an initial drop in the number of undocumented immigrants in the country. However, the number of undocumented immigrants from Mexico soon surged again. When the newly legal immigrants tried to bring their families to the United States, they were often unsuccessful. The families were faced with long waiting lists for visas, so some opted to enter the United States without documentation.

 JOSE

PERSONAL STORIES

At the age of 24, Jose was living in Orlando, Florida. He came to the United States at age five and didn't learn until age 15 that he was there illegally. As a young child, he said his life was like any other child's—filled with school and friends. But as he became a teenager, he learned the difficulty that being an unauthorized immigrant brought. "I never knew being illegal holds you back from many things you can do here in the States....I couldn't get a normal job or even go to school or even get my first car. It is hard and it keeps getting harder for some reason. I don't really know where to turn to."

Parts of the United States–Mexico border are already fenced, but President Trump wants to build a wall along its entire length.

BUILDING A WALL

In 2006, President George W. Bush ordered the construction of more than 600 miles (965 km) of fencing along the United States–Mexico border. The fence was part of an attempt to control the number of undocumented immigrants flooding in from Mexico. It was not terribly effective, though, given that the entire border is about 2,000 miles (3,220 km), so Bush's fence only covered slightly less than a third of it. Unauthorized immigrants simply hired a guide, commonly known as a coyote, to bring them across the border, often in a remote area like the Arizona desert, where there was no fence.

UNDOCUMENTED MEXICAN IMMIGRATION TODAY

Undocumented Mexican immigrants make up the largest segment of unauthorized immigrants in the United States. However, the growth rate of this segment of the population is slowing, having been overtaken by the growth in the number of undocumented Asian immigrants in the United States.

CHAPTER 2

IMMIGRATION FROM ASIA

For many years, the majority of undocumented immigrants came to the United States from Mexico. That trend is changing today. The total number of Mexican and Central American unauthorized immigrants is still higher than the number of unauthorized immigrants from Asia, but the rate of undocumented immigrants from Asia has grown rapidly in recent years. Between 2000 and 2013, Asian undocumented immigration increased by 202 percent.

The history of immigrants from Asia coming to the United States is long and complex, and there have been numerous immigration laws enacted along the way. Immigrants first came over from Asia in large numbers in the mid-nineteenth century. They were inspired by the Gold Rush and the availability of work on the Transcontinental Railroad. At the time, it was legal for them to immigrate. However, it wouldn't be long before laws were put in place to prevent immigration from some Asian countries, particularly China.

Chinese immigrants came to the United States in large numbers around the time of the Gold Rush.

CHINESE IMMIGRATION IN THE MID-1800s

The Gold Rush, which began in California in 1848, brought in an influx of immigrants from China. Many of the Chinese immigrants who came over at this time came to work in the gold mines or as prospectors on their own. If they didn't find success there, many went to work building the Transcontinental Railroad instead. At first, the railroad companies were prejudiced against Chinese immigrants and did not want to hire them. As the companies became desperate for workers, they began hiring Chinese immigrants. The railroad companies paid Chinese immigrants very little money for extremely dangerous work.

PREJUDICE AGAINST CHINESE IMMIGRANTS

Americans were largely xenophobic and racist towards Chinese immigrants. By law, Chinese immigrants were allowed to come to America. But when they arrived, many experienced intense discrimination from Americans. In the four years from 1848 to 1852, the Chinese immigrant population on the West Coast grew from 400 to 25,000 people. As racial tensions grew, Chinese immigrants were subject to violent acts and even lynchings. Americans formed organizations such as the Asiatic Exclusion League to keep Chinese immigrants out of the country.

WORKPLACE DISCRIMINATION

By 1868, Chinese immigrants made up 80 percent of the Central Pacific Railroad workforce. They were paid less than their white co-workers and were often given more dangerous tasks. White laborers were provided with shelter and meals, but Chinese immigrants were forced to provide for themselves.

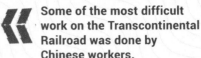

Some of the most difficult work on the Transcontinental Railroad was done by Chinese workers.

RESTRICTING CHINESE IMMIGRATION

Chinese immigrants continued to come to the United States for work, despite the persistent xenophobia. Eventually, the government stepped in, but it wasn't to help the Asian immigrants. Instead, it was to limit the numbers of Asian immigrants coming to the United States.

On the surface, the Page Act, passed by Congress in 1875, seemed like it might help Asian immigrants. It barred them from coming to the United States for jobs in forced labor (when people are forced to work against their will). But if the immigrants didn't have jobs in forced labor, many had no way to get to the United States. Chinese immigrants weren't allowed to come to the United States to look for work; they had to have a job waiting for them. For many, that had been jobs in forced labor.

It was a terrible situation, but for some Asian immigrants, forced labor was the only ticket they had to the United States. The Page Act meant they no longer had that. In 1882, Congress prohibited nearly all immigration from China when it passed the Chinese Exclusion Act. Immigration for Chinese citizens didn't really open up again until 1943.

JAPANESE IMMIGRATION

Some of the first Japanese immigrants to the United States entered illegally—though not by United States laws. Rather, it was illegal by Japanese laws. The Hawaiian consul was aware of a need for laborers in Hawaii, so they secretly brought over 148 Japanese contract laborers.

This took place in 1868, almost two decades after Chinese immigrants began coming to the United States to work in the gold mines. Before that time, Japan had been very isolated, with emigration very strictly controlled. It had been a feudal state, but when Emperor Meiji came to power in 1867, Japan underwent a series of significant political and social changes that are collectively referred to as the Meiji Restoration.

Hawaii experienced an influx of Japanese immigrants after the Meiji Restoration.

LEAVING JAPAN

Once the capitalist system under Emperor Meiji was in place, Japanese people began to consider emigrating. The changes had left many Japanese workers jobless and others with a significant loss in wages. Unfortunately, the option to leave Japan was not immediately available to them by legal means, as strict emigration policies were still in place.

That first group of Japanese laborers brought to Hawaii were discovered and returned to Japan, because they had violated Japanese emigration laws. But by the 1880s, emigration policies had eased, and Japanese immigrants began to legally move to the United States. However, the Japanese government took an active role in selecting which citizens would be allowed to emigrate.

MASS MIGRATION

More than 400,000 Japanese citizens immigrated to the United States between 1886 and 1911. In general, they tended to go to Hawaii or to the Pacific Coast, which are the places closest geographically to Japan. Japanese immigration continued at a significant pace until the early 1920s. In fact, by 1923, Japanese immigrants made up the largest segment of Hawaii's population. Indigenous Hawaiians made up only 16 percent of the population, whereas in 1853 they had made up 97 percent of the population!

 Many of the Japanese who immigrated to Hawaii were former soldiers.

LIVING CONDITIONS

When the mass Japanese migration started, Hawaii wasn't yet a state or even an official United States territory. However, U.S. businesses dominated the island economy, so when Japanese and other Asian immigrants came to the islands, they were essentially coming to the United States.

 Like these sisal cutters, many arrivals from Japan found work on Hawaii's plantations.

The Japanese immigrants worked on plantations, doing backbreaking labor in the fields. The living conditions were often unsanitary, and the laborers were heavily fined or whipped for offenses as minor as talking or standing up to stretch. They were working under a form of indentured servitude. Many could not withstand the harsh conditions and ended up fleeing to the mainland—which put them in violation of their contract and made them unauthorized immigrants. If they were caught, they could be put in jail.

The Japanese immigrants who fled to the mainland generally ended up on the Pacific coast, since it was the closest to Hawaii. They found the same problem as Chinese immigrants—xenophobia, which led them to fear racially motivated violence.

RESTRICTIONS ON JAPANESE IMMIGRATION

Although the first Japanese immigrants came to the United States not long after the Chinese began arriving for the Gold Rush, the number of Japanese immigrants on the Pacific coast didn't really begin to grow until the early twentieth century. Before that, the majority of Japanese immigrants had settled in Hawaii. But by the early 1900s, more Japanese were heading straight to the Pacific coast, and Japanese immigrants unhappy with the labor and living conditions in Hawaii were fleeing to the coast.

On the mainland, the Japanese faced the same discrimination the Chinese had. Americans saw the Japanese as "other" and called them a threat to American workers and to American women, and accused them of corrupting American citizens. Japanese workers were banned from union membership in the American Federation of Labor. Legislators even began to threaten to pass a Japanese Exclusion Act in Congress. In 1908, the Japanese government agreed to limit the number of Japanese emigrating to the United States, and in exchange the United States agreed to allow Japanese immigrants already residing in the United States to bring their immediate family over.

OWNING LAND

Many Japanese and Chinese immigrants settled in California. In 1913, that state passed the California Alien Land Law, which made all undocumented immigrants ineligible for citizenship and land ownership—even if they had purchased land years before. The law was written to discourage immigration of Chinese, Indian, and Korean immigrants, but it was primarily targeted at the Japanese.

The law had a few loopholes in it, which were closed when the California Alien Land Law of 1920 was passed. Undocumented immigrants had been allowed to lease land under the 1913 act, for a period of up to three years, but the 1920 act made that illegal as well.

THE ATTACK ON PEARL HARBOR

On December 7, 1941, a date President Franklin D. Roosevelt said "will live in infamy," the Japanese navy mounted a surprise attack on the U.S. naval base at Pearl Harbor in Hawaii. This event was the catalyst that drove the United States into World War II.

The Japanese attack wasn't so much a direct strike against the United States as an effort to keep the country from interfering in their military actions. The Japanese had a number of military actions planned in the Pacific region, and they wanted to neutralize the U.S. Navy as much as possible before they began.

The Pearl Harbor attack made Americans suspicious of Japanese people living in the United States, resulting in an increase in discrimination against Japanese people.

EFFECTS OF THE ATTACK

The attack inflicted huge losses on the ships of the U.S. Navy's Pacific fleet. In addition, 188 aircraft were destroyed, and more than 2,400 Americans were killed, with more than 1,100 wounded. The next day, the United States declared war on Japan. The U.S. government also forced Japanese Americans—both U.S. citizens and residents without citizenship—into internment camps. On the West Coast, more than 110,000 Japanese Americans were forced into these camps.

The Manzanar Relocation Center in California was just one of the internment camps set up by the government.

INTERNSHIP IN HAWAII

In Hawaii, where the concentration of Japanese Americans was highest in the United States, fewer than 2,000 people were interned. Perhaps the reason for this is that Japanese Americans made up a large percentage of the population in Hawaii—at the time of the attack on Pearl Harbor, there were more than 150,000 Japanese Americans living on the islands, and they made up more than a third of the population. They were definitely not a minority group, and they had been in Hawaii long enough to have established some roots.

MINORITY GROUP

The internment camps were largely fueled by existing racism and xenophobia directed at Japanese Americans. On the West Coast, Japanese Americans were a minority. California and the West Coast have been diversely populated for centuries, but at that time, the Japanese American population in the region was small. There were estimated to be 110,000 Japanese Americans living along the West Coast, and at that time California alone had 6.9 million residents. That means even if every Japanese American on the West Coast was living in California (which wasn't the case—they lived in Oregon and Washington, too), they would still only have represented 1.5 percent of the population in the region.

JAPANESE IMMIGRANTS DENIED CITIZENSHIP

At the time, Japanese immigrants weren't allowed to become citizens. Their descendants could if they were born in the United States, but the original immigrants from Japan weren't able to. And so, at this time, many of the Japanese immigrants weren't technically unauthorized, but they also weren't given the chance to become citizens, either.

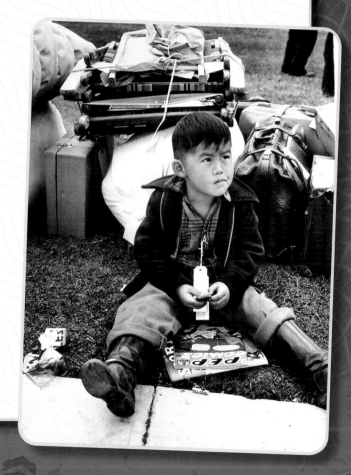

Internees could take some of their belongings to the camps, but had to leave the rest behind.

CHAPTER 3

UNDOCUMENTED IMMIGRANTS TODAY

In the past, there was a somewhat hazy definition of what constituted an undocumented immigrant. Some immigrants to the United States arrived in an clearly unauthorized fashion— they crossed the border in secret or came into the country with false paperwork. Others arrived in a legal fashion but still remained undocumented. One such example of this is a Japanese immigrant arriving under a contract for indentured servitude, but fleeing these horrific conditions to another location in the United States.

Today, immigration laws are far more black-and-white than they were in the past, but it is still possible for immigrants to arrive and live in the U.S. without documentation.

COUNTRIES OF ORIGIN

According to the Migration Policy Institute, the top five countries of birth for undocumented immigrants are Mexico (with 56 percent), Guatemala (with 6 percent), El Salvador (with 4 percent), and Honduras and China (with 3 percent each).

EXPIRED VISAS

The U.S. Immigration and Naturalization Service has estimated that 41 percent of the unauthorized immigrants in the United States today enter the country under a legal visa, such as a student, tourist, or temporary work visa. However, they do not leave the country when the visa expires. They simply remain in the United States past the expiration date, and the government doesn't have the resources to spend time keeping track of them all.

 Students account for a significant number of the immigrants currently living in the United States.

The number of unauthorized immigrants who enter the country on a visa but stay past the visa's expiration has stayed relatively steady since 1982. There was a bit of a spike in the numbers in 2000, but in general it has remained fairly steady, according to data published by the Center for Migration Studies. However, the Pew Research Center and the Migration Policy Institute both feel the number is probably higher than 41 percent. The Migration Policy Institute estimates it as high as 50 percent.

STATES WITH THE MOST IMMIGRANTS

As of 2014, the five U.S. states with the greatest population of immigrants were:
- *California (10.5 million immigrants)*
- *Texas (4.5 million immigrants)*
- *New York (4.5 million immigrants)*
- *Florida (4 million immigrants)*
- *New Jersey (2 million immigrants)*

ENTERING WITHOUT A VISA

Other undocumented immigrants enter the country secretly, without any kind of visa. While the number of immigrants overstaying their visas has remained steady, the number of unauthorized immigrants entering the country without inspection has plummeted in recent years.

The number of immigrants in this category remained relatively steady from 1982 to 1998, and then spiked sharply in 2000. After that, it began to decline quickly and was at a low by 2012. It is difficult to pin down an exact number for how many unauthorized immigrants enter the country in any given year, because they aren't entering through official, countable channels. But based on one method of estimation, it's thought that approximately 674,000 people entered without documentation in 2015.

STATES WITH THE HIGHEST PROPORTION OF IMMIGRANTS

Some states have a significantly larger population of immigrants, in relation to their overall population. As of 2014, the five states with the highest percentage of immigrant population were California (27 percent immigrants), New York (23 percent), New Jersey (22 percent), Florida (20 percent), and Nevada (19 percent).

Immigrants have been known to cross the border without authorization in small planes being used to transport contraband.

WAYS OF GETTING IN

The undocumented immigrants who enter the country without inspection may do so by air. Air traffic controllers keep pretty close tabs on what's going on in the skies, but there are tiny airstrips used without authorization. In theory, an immigrant could pay for a flight into the country and hop off a small plane.

Many people who attempt to cross borders without documentation by land are apprehended. According to the Migration Policy Institute, between October 2015 and February 2016, the United States Border Patrol apprehended 23,553 unaccompanied children and 27,664 families along the border in the southwestern United States. Most were from Mexico, El Salvador, Guatemala, and Honduras.

In total, there are hundreds of thousands of apprehensions of unauthorized immigrants per year. The Migration Policy Institute reported that in 2014, U.S. Customs and Border Protection and U.S. Immigration and Customs Enforcement apprehended 679,996 unauthorized immigrants attempting to enter the United States. A staggering 479,371 of those were at the southwest border (where California, Arizona, New Mexico, and Texas border Mexico). More than half of those apprehended were from Mexico.

STATES WITH THE FASTEST IMMIGRANT GROWTH

Some states act almost as magnets for immigrants, often for geographic reasons. From 2000 to 2014, the two states with the greatest growth in immigrant population were California and Texas (with 1.6 million each)—both of which border Mexico. Close behind was Florida, the gateway to the Caribbean, with 1.3 million. It was followed by New York (with 597,000), and New Jersey (with 484,000).

CHANGES IN NUMBERS

The number of undocumented immigrants entering the United States goes up and down. It dropped when the United States was in an economic recession from roughly 2005 to 2009. Once the economy rebounded, the numbers began to climb again, and they are currently near record levels. Whether that trend will continue under Donald Trump's presidency remains to be seen. President Donald Trump has publicly talked about his plan to build a physical wall between the United States and Mexico. The wall is an attempt to lower the number of undocumented immigrants entering the United States.

During his campaign, Donald Trump promised that he would crack down on undocumented immigration.

Unauthorized Immigrant Demographics

According to the Department of Homeland Security's Office of Immigration Statistics, as of 2012 there were an estimated 11.4 million unauthorized immigrants living in the United States. More than half of those undocumented immigrants were living in just four states: 28 percent were living in California, 13 percent in Texas, 8 percent in New York, and 5 percent in Florida.

The breakdown of where unauthorized immigrants are living is not terribly surprising. Both California and Texas share a border with Mexico and have fairly large farming and ranching enterprises where undocumented immigrants can easily find work. Florida is only about 90 miles from Cuba, so many Cubans fleeing the country's communist government travel to Florida. New York is a huge melting pot with an incredibly diverse population—a place where immigrants may find a sense of community.

STATES WITH THE LARGEST GROWTH PERCENTAGE OF IMMIGRANTS

From 2000 to 2014, the five states where the percentage of growth of the immigrant population was the highest were Tennessee and Kentucky (which grew by 102 percent each), Wyoming (which grew by 101 percent), North Dakota (which grew by 99 percent), and South Carolina (which grew by 97 percent). These states have historically had very small foreign-born populations, so even a small increase in immigrant population means a big jump in growth.

COUNTRY OF ORIGIN

The Migration Policy Institute estimates that about 71 percent were born in Mexico or Central America. About 14 percent are from Asia, and about 6 percent are from South America. Another 4 percent are from Europe, Canada, or Oceania, and 3 percent are from Africa. Only 2 percent come from the Caribbean, despite its proximity to Florida.

Although undocumented immigrants of today tend to be better educated than the ones who came over in generations past, they still tend to have a lower education level than U.S. citizens and legal immigrants. For example, only 51 percent of undocumented immigrants have completed high school, compared to 75 percent of legal immigrants. Still, they are often able to find work in the United States. They tend to be paid less than citizens and legal immigrants. They often find work in agriculture, construction, and the service, installation, and repair industries.

Undocumented immigrants often end up in the construction field, where they sometimes work for lower pay than U.S. citizens.

CHILDREN OF ILLEGAL IMMIGRANTS

From 2009 to 2013, 5.1 million children under the age of 18 in the United States lived with at least one parent who was an undocumented immigrant. The majority of these children were U.S. citizens, but 19 percent were also undocumented themselves.

Anyone born in the United States automatically becomes a U.S. citizen. The current interpretation of the Constitution is that babies born to undocumented immigrant parents are U.S. citizens from birth, as long as they were born within the United States. This can be a sticky situation, because the undocumented parent(s) of the child could be deported back to their home country, even though their child has the right to stay.

These children live with the fear that their parents may, at any time, be deported. For that reason, these families are often extremely hesitant to report crimes against them, to seek medical help at a hospital, or to do anything that could draw attention to them and result in the parents getting deported.

Having a baby who is a U.S. citizen does not give an undocumented immigrant the right to stay.

 MAYRA

Eight-year-old Mayra spends her days in Minnesota going to the park, swimming, and playing with her siblings. But while she and two of her siblings are U.S. citizens, her parents are both undocumented immigrants from Guatemala. As much as Mayra dreams of her future as a pop star, she dreams even more of a future where her parents can live without fear of deportation.

PERSONAL STORIES

HUMAN TRAFFICKING

Not everyone who enters the country without documentation does so by choice. The U.S. Department of State reports that around 17,000 people are brought into the United States each year through human trafficking. Human trafficking is the illegal transportation (by force) of a person for the purposes of making them work in forced labor or prostitution.

Victims of human trafficking may be deceived by the fake promise of a good job. When they arrive, they are put to work in sweatshops, domestic servitude, or the sex trade. Often, there is no way the people could alert the authorities to their situation even if they wanted to. Some wouldn't try even if they could, because they are afraid of being deported. As undocumented immigrants, they have very few rights.

HOW MANY VICTIMS?

Exact numbers are difficult to pinpoint, since many trafficked people are living under the radar—they may be held prisoner, or they may simply be living very quietly to avoid deportation. But the International Labor Organization estimates that at least 12.3 million people worldwide are working in forced labor at any given time, and 2.4 million of them are doing so because they were victims of human trafficking. In the United States, it is estimated that at least 10,000 people are working in forced labor at any given time.

HUMAN TRAFFICKERS

PERSONAL STORIES

Human traffickers operate all around the world. One human trafficker, Aroldo Castillo-Serrano, smuggled more than 40 Guatemalans to the United States and forced them to work 12-hour days. They lived in cramped conditions and were told they had to work to pay off a debt to Castillo-Serrano. This trafficker had a partner, Ana Angelica Pedro Juan, who would force the workers to hand over their paychecks and threaten to harm their families if they tried to refuse.

 Human trafficking is a problem that is getting more attention these days from organizations like the United Nations.

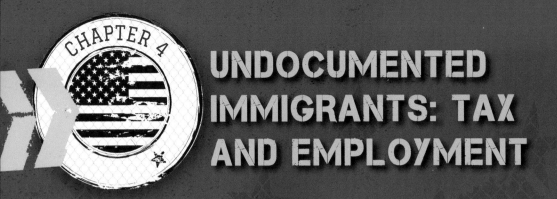

CHAPTER 4

UNDOCUMENTED IMMIGRANTS: TAX AND EMPLOYMENT

"Give me your tired, your poor,
Your huddled masses yearning to breathe free,
The wretched refuse of your teeming shore.
Send these, the homeless, tempest-tost to me,
I lift my lamp beside the golden door."

So read the words of the poet Emma Lazarus, which are inscribed on a plaque on the Statue of Liberty's pedestal. And indeed, for many years the people of the United States have proudly described their country as a "melting pot" that is welcoming to foreigners. However, racism and ethnocentrism still exist in the United States, and they are sometimes directed at immigrants.

Undocumented immigrants face a particular stigma. This may be partly because some American citizens have preconceived notions about the benefits undocumented immigrants are getting from residing in the United States. While some of these notions are rooted in truth, many turn out to be false.

TAX ASSUMPTIONS

When people argue for deporting undocumented immigrants, one argument that many of them cite is their belief that undocumented immigrants don't pay taxes. This belief probably comes from an old model of undocumented immigration, where immigrants came into the United States without documentation and took jobs that would pay them under the table. They worked for cash and paid no taxes.

However, the model of undocumented immigration has changed quite a bit. In 1986, Congress passed the Immigration Reform and Control Act, which was an attempt to crack down on the hiring of undocumented immigrants. The Immigration Reform and Control Act was supposed to work by making it illegal for employers to knowingly hire unauthorized immigrants. This meant that unauthorized immigrants who wanted to work had to find false documentation. A market for fake Social Security cards, birth certificates, and other forms of ID grew quickly.

Undocumented immigrants could get a fake Social Security card so that they could pretend to their employers that they were legal residents in the United States. According to Stephen Goss, Chief Actuary of the Social Security Administration, in 2010 an estimated 1.8 million immigrants were working under fake or stolen Social Security cards. He estimates that by 2040, that number will likely have reached 3.4 million.

The numbers provided by the Social Security Administration are used to prove eligibility.

SOCIAL SECURITY ADMINISTRATION

PAYING SOCIAL SECURITY

Whether the employers actually believe the Social Security card and number are valid is irrelevant. They are adhering to the letter of the law by requiring an employee to provide one. Some employers who hire immigrants are well aware that the card may be a fake, and they simply look the other way.

The result, in any case, is that immigrants who gain employment in the United States by using a fake Social Security card actually end up paying taxes. They simply pay taxes on an identity that doesn't exist! In fact, numerous 2016 reports stated that undocumented immigrants pay about $12 billion in taxes every year, by virtue of paying under fake Social Security numbers. When a tax payment comes in, if the federal government finds that the Social Security number isn't linked to anyone they have on file, they simply put the money in a fund called the Earnings Suspense File. Eventually, much of that money goes to pay out Social Security benefits to American citizens.

HOW MUCH DO THEY PAY?

Stephen Goss's calculations showed that in 2010, the 1.8 million immigrants working under fake or stolen Social Security numbers contributed $13 billion to the Social Security system. In 2013, he stated, "We estimate that earnings by unauthorized immigrants result in a net positive effect on Social Security financial status generally, and that this effect contributed roughly $12 billion to the cash flow of the program for 2010." By Goss's calculations, then, undocumented immigrants were adding to the system and taking very little out.

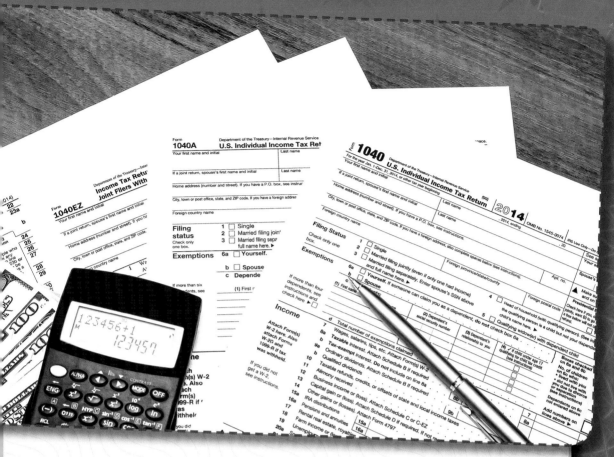

WHO BENEFITS?

By having a fake Social Security card, undocumented immigrants pay into the Social Security system, even though they won't benefit from it. Undocumented immigrants who never become naturalized citizens will never be eligible to collect Social Security benefits, because Social Security is offered only to United States citizens. So even if they spent years paying into the system, they will get nothing back. In addition to having fake Social Security numbers, at least half of undocumented immigrants file tax returns, according to the Institute on Taxation and Economic Policy. Even those who don't file a tax return may have taxes deducted from their paychecks. The belief that undocumented immigrants do not pay taxes is therefore inaccurate.

Many undocumented immigrants file a tax return every year, even if they get little in return.

THE ITIN SYSTEM

In 1996, the government instituted the ITIN (Individual Taxpayer Identification Number) program. It may have been a response to the realization that efforts to limit the number of unauthorized immigrants in the job market were backfiring. Under the ITIN program, a person who cannot obtain a valid Social Security number can instead be issued an ITIN. They use the ITIN in order to file taxes. The ITIN program has actually brought in significant revenue for the government. In 2010, the government gained about $870 million in tax revenue from the roughly 3 million people who used an ITIN to pay income taxes!

 The ITIN program has given undocumented immigrants a way to pay taxes without risking deportation.

PROTECTION UNDER ITIN

According to federal tax law, the Internal Revenue Service cannot share data with the Department of Homeland Security. This means that if an undocumented immigrant uses an ITIN, it cannot then be used to identify and subsequently deport them. The ITIN is only used for tax purposes. In some cases, it might also help an immigrant obtain citizenship, because a history of paying taxes can help immigrants prove their desire to obtain legal citizenship.

TAX AS A CAMPAIGN ISSUE

This subject of undocumented immigrants and taxes was often in the news in 2016, because of statements made by Donald Trump during his presidential campaign. One of his campaign promises was that if elected, he would change immigration enforcement to fix the supposed problem of undocumented immigrants in the United States. One of the statements he made on the campaign trail was that undocumented immigrants were claiming $4.2 billion in tax credits. Not surprisingly, this frustrated U.S. citizens who believed it to be true. However, it was later proven to be false.

In an amusing twist, it seems that undocumented immigrants may actually pay more into the tax system than President Trump, the very person who accused them of not paying. Trump may not have paid federal taxes for a period of 18 years, which is legal due to various loopholes in tax laws. At the same time, the Institute on Taxation & Economic Policy (ITEP) reported the nearly $12 billion figure that undocumented immigrants have paid into the tax system.

TAX REVENUES FROM UNDOCUMENTED IMMIGRANTS

Undocumented immigrants pay about $11.64 billion in taxes each year, but it is not all income tax. This figure breaks down as $6.9 billion in sales and excise taxes, $3.6 billion in property taxes, and $1.1 billion in personal income tax.

THE BEST SOLUTION?

Donald Trump's promises to crack down on immigration won him a lot of support. During the 2016 presidential campaign, Democratic nominee Hillary Clinton suggested that a better solution to the issue of undocumented immigrants was granting them a path to citizenship. This means providing a way to gain legal status in the country where they live.

While there are many different opinions on the issue, one thing is certain. According to ITEP, if the 11 million undocumented immigrants currently living in the United States were granted citizenship, their tax contributions would increase by an estimated $2.1 billion per year.

 Democratic presidential nominee Hillary Clinton had very different ideas on immigration than Donald Trump.

EMPLOYMENT ASSUMPTIONS

Many U.S. citizens have assumptions about the taxes that undocumented immigrants pay, and just as many have assumptions about their impact on the job market. Some U.S. citizens think that illegal immigrants take so-called good jobs from Americans. In reality, undocumented immigrants are more likely to take jobs that U.S. citizens aren't particularly interested in. In this way, they fill a hole in the job market.

In the past several decades, more U.S. citizens have pursued higher education, which opens up more job possibilities. College-educated young adults typically tend toward office and professional jobs, as well as sales and management. These young adults typically do not want low-paying labor jobs or jobs in the service industry. But these jobs are necessary in the economy.

A significant number of undocumented Asian immigrants work in the food industry.

In past generations, young adults who did not pursue higher education generally took these jobs, but in recent decades, fewer young adults have been interested in these types of jobs. However, many undocumented immigrants typically are willing to do them. It can be difficult for undocumented immigrants to find work for a variety of reasons, including lack of education, lack of fluency in English, or their undocumented status. Undocumented immigrants are generally willing to fill those same types of jobs that Americans tend to avoid.

JOBS FOR CITIZENS AND IMMIGRANTS WITHOUT DIPLOMAS

There are many people who don't complete high school—both U.S. citizens and immigrants. However, the jobs they pursue can be different, depending on their status. The three most popular jobs for American-born workers who don't have a diploma are cashier, truck driver, and janitor. However, the top three jobs for immigrant workers who don't have a diploma are maid, cook, and agricultural worker.

ONE UNDOCUMENTED IMMIGRANT'S SUCCESS STORY

CASE STUDY

In 1970, a 25-year-old mother of five from Guatemala could not feed her children. Her husband did not make enough money to provide for their family, and when the young mother asked his boss for money to buy milk, he threw 13 cents at her and told her never to return. Desperate, she left her children with her mother and joined eight friends who were attempting to immigrate to the United States. She promised her mother she would return for the children.

The group traveled to Mexico but were denied visas to enter the United States, so they hired a coyote to take them across the border. The entire group was caught by immigration police when the coyote attempted to sexually assault the young mother, and a member of the group tried to rescue her. They were jailed in Chula Vista, California, for a month, where the mother got very sick and fell into a coma. When she recovered, she was sent back to Guatemala.

Two years later, after working to save money in Guatemala, she tried to cross the border with a coyote again. This time, she succeeded and got a job as a live-in housekeeper for a family in Sherman Oaks, California, making $30 per week.

She later moved to New Jersey and worked as a housekeeper, saving enough money to bring her five children to the United States. This undocumented immigrant's children are now all grown business owners and licensed professionals. She is now a U.S. citizen herself. Even though she is well past retirement age, she works seven days a week at the commercial cleaning business she owns.

Poverty and crime are widespread in Guatemala, pushing some Guatemalans to immigrate to the United States.

Harmful Stereotypes

Some Americans have prejudiced beliefs about immigrants' work ethic. They believe that immigrants are lazy or do not want to work hard. This is an unfortunate continuation of the racist and xenophobic stereotypes employers held against immigrants in the mid-nineteenth century. Of course, it is both inaccurate and harmful to make assumptions about people based on their country of origin.

Many immigrants end up finding great success and prosperity in the United States.

CHAPTER 5

CULTURAL IDENTITY

Negative assumptions about tax status and employment are not the only forms of prejudice many undocumented immigrants experience. They are also faced with people making assumptions about their effect on crime and public safety. Further, many Americans believe that immigrants do not want to assimilate to American culture and are angered by this.

Although the divide isn't as strict as it once was, immigrants still tend to live grouped in certain neighborhoods. And when an immigrant family moves into a neighborhood dominated by an ethnicity other than their own, they often face discrimination. This can result in Mexican immigrants staying in predominantly Mexican neighborhoods, Asian immigrants staying in predominantly Asian neighborhoods, and so on.

IMMIGRANT COMMUNITIES

When people stay in their own neighborhood, sometimes there is little need to assimilate into American culture. For example, a Chinese immigrant living in Chinatown in a major city may not have an urgent need to learn English. Many people in their neighborhood speak a Chinese dialect, so they can generally get all of their needs met without speaking English.

Immigrants bring their culture and customs with them, creating a great deal of diversity.

This is true even of smaller populations of immigrants. For example, there are certain sections of Los Angeles where many Armenian immigrants live. These areas are informally known as "Little Armenia," and even business signs and street signs are written in Armenian. Particularly for the older, non-working immigrants, there is no real need to learn English and venture beyond the comfort of Little Armenia.

CRIME AND PUBLIC SAFETY

On the campaign trail in 2016, Donald Trump made a statement that fueled another stereotype about undocumented immigrants—that they result in more crime in the United States. At a speech in Phoenix—a city with a high immigrant population because of its proximity to Mexico—Trump announced that if his opponent, Hillary Clinton, were elected, it would encourage more undocumented immigration, which would result in "thousands of more violent, horrible crimes, and total chaos and lawlessness."

This statement touched on an assumption and fear many Americans feel towards undocumented immigrants. They believe that when undocumented immigrants arrive, they bring crime with them. As it turns out, these assumptions are untrue.

CHECKING THE FACTS

Communities with high immigrant concentrations actually tend to have lower crime rates than other areas. Harvard University sociologist Robert Sampson is the former scientific director of the Project on Human Development in Chicago Neighborhoods. In his 2012 book *Great American City*, he stated that an increase in immigration in Chicago during the 1990s resulted in decreases in neighborhood homicide rates. A 2013 study in Los Angeles found similar results, and a 2014 study of 157 metropolitan areas found that violent crime decreased when immigrant population rose.

One possible reason for this is that immigrants tend to move into lower-cost neighborhoods that have been ravaged by poverty and crime. They then revitalize these neighborhoods by opening businesses in vacant storefronts, which leaves the area less likely to experience crime. Another theory says that undocumented immigrants tend to avoid behavior that might attract the police, since they fear deportation, so they live law-abiding lives. And yet another possibility is simply that the majority of immigrants are ambitious, hardworking people who moved their family to a new country for a better life.

Chicago's Chinatown is the second-largest Chinatown in the United States.

BY THE NUMBERS: IMMIGRANTS AND CRIME

Whatever the reason, the numbers don't lie. Between 1990 and 2010, the number of illegal immigrants in the United States tripled. Over that same period, the rate of violent and property crimes both declined by more than 40 percent. One study found that from 1999 to 2006, crime rates were lowest in the states that had the highest increase in immigrant populations. And during that same time period, the crime rate dropped 14 percent in the 19 states with the highest number of immigrants, while crime fell only 7 percent in the other 31 states.

ASSIMILATING TO AMERICAN CULTURE

Some American citizens believe that immigrants don't want to assimilate to American culture. Part of this has to do with language barriers. Many immigrants come to the United States with a limited command of English. Some Americans take that as a sign that they don't want to learn English. In reality, most immigrant families strongly

Immigrants can take English classes to help them better participate in American life.

encourage their children to learn English along with their native tongue. As for the older generations in the family, if they do wish to learn English, they may run into difficulty because there is not enough adult ESL instruction available to meet the ever-growing demand for it.

VINCENT CHIN

PERSONAL STORIES

Vincent Chin was born in China, but he was raised by Chinese American parents in a middle-class neighborhood in suburban Detroit. At the age of 27, he was working as an industrial draftsman during the week, waiting tables on weekends, and was engaged to be married. On a June evening, he went to a club with friends to celebrate his bachelor party. He was attacked by two white auto industry workers who blamed him for the layoffs in the auto industry. They assumed he was of Japanese descent, and at the time Japanese auto manufacturers were selling more cars in the United States, leading to a downturn in the American auto industry.

Chin left the club, but the two attackers tracked him down at a nearby McDonald's, where they beat him to death. He was a Chinese American man and a U.S. citizen. He grew up going to American schools and speaking English. He went to the same clubs as any American in that region. Yet his white attackers still made prejudice assumptions about him based on his race and violently attacked and murdered him.

Asian immigrants and American citizens of Asian descent may still experience prejudice today.

Like the German immigrants of the 1900s, Italian immigrants created communities in American cities, like this one in Mulberry Street in New York City's Little Italy.

THE CULTURAL EFFECTS OF COLONIZATION

The English colonists brought their customs and language to North America when they colonized the lands of Native Americans. The Native Americans had (and have) many cultures and languages. Colonists established their own culture and language as dominant, often through military force. Despite the fact that immigrants from many countries came to North America, English culture and customs became dominant—making them the standard by which assimilation was measured.

CULTURAL IDENTITY

Many immigrants have a desire to hold onto the cultures and customs of their home country. This is not a new phenomenon. Over a century ago, German immigrants settled in particular neighborhoods and held onto their language, foods, and culture to remind them of their home. Italian immigrants did the same. So did Irish immigrants. The customs, foods, and languages immigrants bring with them often enrich the culture of their new country.

IMMIGRANT INFLUENCE ON AMERICAN CULTURE

A significant population of Americans feel that immigrants aren't trying hard enough to assimilate. For example, a 2015 study indicated that 59 percent of Americans think that immigrants don't learn English fast enough. But is it fair to decide that American-born citizens should be the ones to define the cultural mainstream in a nation that has an incredibly rich, diverse immigrant population?

 The Mexican holiday of Cinco de Mayo commemorates a battle from 1862. In the United States, it has become a festival of Mexican culture.

Over the years, immigrants have influenced American culture and customs. Mexican food is incredibly popular and widespread, particularly in the west and southwest. Italian food is found across the United States. Foods from other nationalities have gained popularity in recent decades, too. Many Americans who are not of Mexican descent celebrate holidays like Cinco de Mayo, and just as many Americans not of Irish descent observe St. Patrick's Day.

If you go back far enough, nearly everything about American culture was influenced by some other culture. So to define American culture simply as what's defined by white Americans is quite limiting—and expecting immigrants to immediately assimilate to that culture is even more limiting.

REFUGEES AND ASYLEES

Refugees are people who come to a country because they are fleeing persecution or because their home country is unsafe due to natural disaster or violent conditions. The United States was flooded with Jewish refugees after World War II, when they were released from concentration camps in Germany and found they had no homes or families to return to.

While many Americans would like to be able to help refugees, they aren't necessarily so sure they want to welcome them into the country. Refugees were a frequent topic of discussion during the 2016 presidential election. Thousands of refugees from war-ravaged Syria were looking for a safe place to relocate, and the United States was divided as to whether to open the country's doors to them. The United States has suffered terrorist attacks from radical groups in the Middle East since the early twenty-first century. Many people feared that allowing Syrian refugees into the United States would also potentially open the door to entry by terrorists.

Syrian refugees have been coming to the United States as their country is torn apart by war.

ADMITTING REFUGEES

Periodically, a foreign country will undergo some sort of strife—such as war or a natural disaster—and refugees will be forced to flee. The United States is often a popular destination. But the United States government sets limits on the numbers of refugees it will accept each year—and which countries it will accept them from.

In Idaho, demonstrators show their support for refugees.

REFUGEES BY THE NUMBERS

According to official government figures, in 2016 the president and Congress determined that the United States would allow 25,000 refugees from Africa, 13,000 from East Asia, 4,000 from Europe and Central Asia, 3,000 from Latin America and the Caribbean, 34,000 from the Near East/ South Asia, and 6,000 under an "unallocated reserve" quota. This makes an overall total of 85,000 refugees allowed in 2016.

THE AL SHARAA FAMILY

Faez al Sharaa was held at gunpoint one day when he left his house in Daraa, Syria, and decided it was time to flee the country. He and his wife spent nearly two years in a refugee camp in Jordan, while they anxiously waited for a country to accept them as refugees. They welcomed their first child while in the refugee camp.

Finally, the family was sent to Dallas, Texas, where their second child was born. Al Sharaa works as a shelf-stocker, while his wife raises their two children. They live in an apartment. The family feels lucky to have escaped Syria with their lives.

PERSONAL STORIES

ASYLEES

People known as asylees make up a similar category of immigrants, but there is one major difference. If a person is currently living in the United States and does not feel they can safely return to their home country, they are considered an asylee. A person applies for refugee status before they leave their home country. However, both refugees and asylees must meet the same criteria to gain entry into the United States. The United States does not have an established quota for how many people can be granted asylum in a given year.

Refugees and asylees are authorized residents. They are in the United States legally, but they do not have citizenship rights. However, if a refugee or asylee lives in the United States for a year, they can then apply for a green card and start the citizenship process.

CHAPTER 6

DEPORTATION AND BORDERS

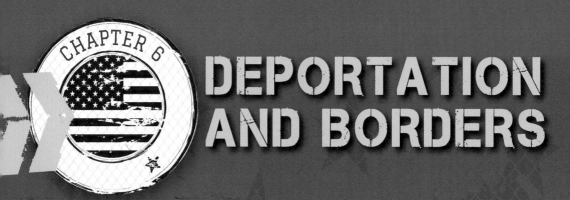

Deportation is the greatest fear of most undocumented immigrants. The vast majority of them came to the United States to better their quality of life, and do not want to be sent back. Fear of deportation is what leads many undocumented immigrants to live under the radar, not even seeking proper medical care when they need it. They don't want to do anything that might alert authorities to their situation.

HOW DEPORTATION WORKS

In general, when Immigration and Customs Enforcement (ICE) identifies an undocumented immigrant and acts upon it, a few things can happen. In many cases, the arresting officer works for ICE. Sometimes a member of state or local police for the area where the undocumented immigrant lives or works arrests the immigrant for a minor criminal act, such as a traffic violation. In a case like this, the arresting officer will book the immigrant, who will then be turned over to ICE. ICE will determine that they are undocumented.

U.S. Customs and Border Patrol officers can also arrest undocumented immigrants. Typically, this happens if an undocumented immigrant is in the process of attempting to cross the border.

RIGHTS FOR ARRESTED IMMIGRANTS

When a member of law enforcement who is not with ICE arrests an undocumented immigrant, the law enforcement agency in question can hold the immigrant for ICE, but only temporarily. ICE officials can file a detainer so that the immigrant is held for a maximum of 48 hours. If ICE is not able to interview the immigrant within that 48 hours, the law enforcement agency must release the immigrant.

Deportation arrests can happen in public, at an individual's home, or at the individual's workplace. Immigrants do not have to let officers into their home without a warrant, but not all immigrants know this. If ICE or the police ask to come into the house and the immigrant allows them to, then the immigrant can be arrested.

If ICE interviews the detained immigrant and determines they want to go forward with deportation, the immigrant is given a Notice to Appear, which is essentially a court summons. In court, a judge who does not work for ICE will preside over the hearing to determine whether the immigrant should indeed be deported. There are certain defenses an immigrant can use that may persuade the judge not to order deportation.

T8031

POLICE
ICE

Undocumented immigrants live in fear of being arrested during ICE raids like this one.

LEAVING THE COUNTRY

Removal proceedings can take months or years, so often an undocumented immigrant isn't immediately deported. In fact, they will only be immediately deported if a prior order of removal exists, or if they sign a deportation agreement or accept voluntary departure.

During the removal proceedings, if an immigrant is granted bond and can pay it, they may be released from custody and allowed to go about their life while waiting for the removal proceedings to be finished.

CLOSING THE BORDERS

In recent years, immigration has become a highly contentious topic. While both presidential candidates in the 2016 campaign spoke at length about immigration, Republican candidate Donald Trump proposed a much more sweeping reform than his Democratic opponent, Hillary Clinton.

Clinton's plan would have largely followed what the Obama administration had put into place. Trump, on the other hand, argued that the United States needed to clamp down on immigration and deport undocumented immigrants as soon as possible. He promised to build a physical wall along the United States–Mexico border, which he claimed Mexico would pay for.

In Arkansas in 2017, Muslims gathered to show support for immigrants.

In some places, refugee camps look more like jails.

These were ambitious claims. Trump ended up winning the election, giving him a chance to try to put his immigration plans into action. However, his plans to clamp down on the borders and enforce immigration bans hit an immediate snag. The executive orders on immigration, which he issued within two weeks of becoming president, were met with much pushback from the U.S. court system, not to mention Congress and large segments of the American public.

Public Opinion on Immigration

There are many factors that influence American-born citizens' opinions on undocumented immigrants. One major factor is the state of the economy. Unemployment has always been an issue in the United States. In good times, unemployment rates are low and people are generally content. There are always people out of work, but the overall economy is stable and most people have gainful employment. At other times, such as during the recession in 2008, unemployment rates are sky-high, and U.S. citizens question how they will provide for their families.

Economic Concerns

The unfortunate reality is that fears about job loss and unemployment sometimes influence American-born citizens' views of immigrants. Americans who are out of work may begin to resent immigrants because they see them as competition for jobs. However, there is no proof that hiring immigrants has a negative effect on the unemployment rate for American citizens. In fact, some estimates say that for every immigrant hired, 1.2 nonimmigrant jobs are created.

Millennials

Millennials—people born between roughly 1980 and 1994—are also often blamed for issues with the economy. Some older people believe that millennials lack the work ethic of previous generations. Critics of the millennial generation argue that they expect success without working hard. Some studies seem to support this view, while others contradict it.

One study has regularly interviewed high school seniors since 1976. So far, the results of their study have shown that millennials are less willing to work overtime than two previous generations (Generation X and the Baby Boomer generation). The results have also shown that compared to Generation X and the Baby Boomers, more millennials would choose not to hold jobs if they had enough money to live without working. However, another survey found that 1992 business school graduates (who would be members of Generation X) expected to work 58 hours a week, while 2012 graduates (millennials) expected to work 72 hours a week.

 A third of millennials between 26 and 33 years old have a four-year college degree or more, making them the best-educated generation in American history.

IMMIGRANTS AND NATIONAL SECURITY

Some people worry about the impact of immigrants on national security. As described earlier, studies show that cities with high immigration populations often experience lower crime rates. However, that is a look at localized crime. What some Americans worry is that welcoming immigrants to the United States invites potential terrorists.

Ever since the attacks of September 11, 2001, Americans have been on edge about terrorist attacks. The events of September 11 were so unexpected and so horrific that many Americans lost their confidence in America as a safe place.

CONFLICTING VIEWS

This collective fear has led some citizens to have a knee-jerk reaction against immigrants. While many Americans remain welcoming to immigrants, others fear that terrorists may attempt to immigrate to the United States to carry out attacks. This leads some Americans to fear all immigrants from the same country or religious background as terrorists who have attacked the United States.

For example, ISIS, one of the main terrorist groups posing a threat to United States national security, is a radical Islamist group—an extremist offshoot of the Muslim faith. ISIS has made numerous threats against the United States and its citizens, and some individuals who have carried out attacks on U.S. soil have claimed to do so in the name of ISIS. Because of this, some U.S. citizens fear that any person of the Muslim faith is a potential terrorist. This is, of course, wholly unwarranted. ISIS is an extremist group that does not represent Islam or its followers. The vast majority of Muslims are faithful, nonviolent people who would never consider planning a terrorist attack against anyone.

Many Americans feel that it is completely unfair to discriminate against Muslims immigrating to the United States. They argue that the vast majority are likely to be nonviolent people who could be a welcome addition to the melting pot that is the United States. But to other Americans, it's just not worth the risk.

The United States has strict screening policies for immigrants wanting to enter the country, but no amount of screening can weed out absolutely all potentially dangerous people. The question is, which is more detrimental to the United States: denying many good people the chance to enter the country, or risking the potential for a few dangerous individuals to slip through?

 The 9/11 attacks, which destroyed part of the Pentagon, made many Americans fearful for their safety.

THE FUTURE OF IMMIGRATION

The future of immigration is unknown. President Trump may or may not actually build a wall, enforce tougher immigration laws, ban Muslim immigrants, or force a registry. If he takes any of these actions, it could have a powerful effect on the undocumented immigrant population. His aim is to lower the undocumented immigrant population. However, when lawmakers have tried to do this in the past, the legislation has sometimes backfired and actually increased the population of undocumented immigrants. Whatever happens, immigration will be a topic of debate for years to come.

 Supporters of Hillary Clinton tended to favor an immigrant-friendly policy.

GLOSSARY

amnesty Official pardon for someone who was convicted of a political offense.

asylee A person seeking or granted political asylum.

Baby Boomer A person born in the years following World War II, when there was an increase in the birth rate in the United States.

Bracero Program A series of laws under which Mexican citizens could work in the United States and be guaranteed minimum wages and basic human rights.

coyote A person who smuggles people across the U.S. border from Mexico in exchange for a fee.

domestic servitude A system in which people work as live-in help for a family, but not for fair wages and conditions—a form of forced labor.

ESL English as a Second Language. ESL speakers spoke another language from birth, and have learned English as a secondary language.

ethnocentrism The belief that one's own culture is superior and that other cultures should be held to the same standards.

feudal A system in which lower-class people work for members of the upper classes in exchange for protection, a place to live, or a share of the product.

forced labor Work that people are forced to do under the threat of punishment.

Generation X The generation of people born after the Baby Boomers, generally from the early 1960s to the late 1970s.

Great Depression A deep economic downturn from 1929 to 1939. It affected many countries, notably the United States. Poverty and joblessness were at record highs.

human trafficking The trade of humans, usually for forced labor or for work in prostitution.

indentured servitude A work arrangement in which one person is contracted to work for another for a set period of time to pay off a debt.

indigenous Native to a particular place.

Internal Revenue Service Federal agency responsible for collecting taxes and enforcing tax laws.

lynched Killed by hanging.

Meiji Restoration A chain of events that returned Japan to imperial rule under Emperor Meiji in 1868.

millennials Generally considered to be people born between 1980 and 1994.

Oceania Islands in the tropical Pacific Ocean. Includes islands in Southeast Asia, Australasia, the Malay Archipelago, and the Americas.

Social Security A social insurance program that covers retirement, disability, and survivors' benefits.

stigma A mark of disgrace.

Transcontinental Railroad A network of railroads that cross a land mass with terminals at different borders.

xenophobia Prejudice against people from other countries.

FOR MORE INFORMATION

BOOKS

Currie, Stephen. *Undocumented Immigrant Youth*. San Diego, CA: ReferencePoint Press, 2016.

Grande, Reyna. *The Distance Between Us*. New York: Aladdin, 2016.

McCormick, Lisa Wade. *Frequently Asked Questions About Growing Up as an Undocumented Immigrant*. New York: The Rosen Publishing Group, 2013.

Nazario, Sonia. *Enrique's Journey: The True Story of a Boy Determined to Reunite With His Mother*. New York: Delacorte Books for Young Readers, 2013.

WEBSITES

Learn about the undocumented immigrant population on this interactive map:
www.migrationpolicy.org/programs/us-immigration-policy-program-data-hub/unauthorized-immigrant-population-profiles

KIND (Kids in Need of Defense) provides an overview of immigration law and relevant agencies:
supportkind.org/wp-content/uploads/2015/04/Chapter-2-Overview-of-Immigration-Law-and-Relevant-Agencies.pdf

The Pew Research Center site has a number of pages devoted to Hispanic population trends in the United States:
www.pewhispanic.org

INDEX